Praise

"A vastly imagined Wonderbook—fearsome, hilarious, familiar and arcane—in which a brilliantly savaged Walmart, both a temple and a tomb, spawns an epidemic of pharonic proportions, exhausting nothing less than everything. An extraordinary experience."
RIKKI DUCORNET, NATIONAL BOOK CRITICS CIRCLE AWARD FINALIST, AUTHOR OF *BRIGHTFELLOW* AND *THE DEEP ZOO*

"In a series of librettos for the end times, a compilation of nearly operatic extent, Lucy Biederman's stage in *The Walmart Book of the Dead* is the size of the world's biggest box-store wherein miles of product attempt to dwarf the lonely figures who journey through its forsaken aisles like refugees from a Denis Johnson fever dream singing their apologetics and choking confusions, insincerities and blunt wonderments, songs of tedium, choking confessions, proprieties of the herd, and much more, arias rising to honor the supremely banal pathos of contemporary post-existence, each song haunting, brief, yet interwoven into a collective performance of current afterlife, funereal yet bright beyond vision. An homage to capitalism."
SKIP FOX, AUTHOR OF *WIRED TO ZONE* AND *SHEER INDEFINITE*

About the Author

Lucy Biederman is a lecturer in English at Case Western Reserve University. She holds a Ph.D. in English from the University of Louisiana-Lafayette and an MFA in creative writing from George Mason University. She has written four chapbooks of poetry, and her short stories, essays, and poems have appeared recently in *Bat City Review*, *The Collagist*, *AGNI*, *Ploughshares*, *Web Conjunctions*, and *Pleiades*. Her scholarship, which has been published in *The Henry James Review*, *Women's Studies*, and elsewhere, focuses on how contemporary American women writers interpret their literary forebears. She shops at Walmart.

Visit Lucy online: *lucybiederman.wordpress.com*

The Walmart Book of the Dead
Copyright © 2017 Lucy Biederman
All rights reserved.

Print Edition
ISBN: 978-1-925417-57-9

Published by Vine Leaves Press 2017
Melbourne, Victoria, Australia

Cover painting by Brendan O'Connell
Cover design by Jessica Bell
Interior design by Amie McCracken

National Library of Australia Cataloguing-in-Publication entry (paperback)
Creator: Biederman, Lucy, author.
Title: The walmart book of the dead / Lucy Biederman.
ISBN: 9781925417586 (paperback)
Subjects: Dead--Fiction.
Spirits--Fiction.
Fantasy fiction.

The
WALMART
BOOK
of the
DEAD

Lucy Biederman

Vine Leaves Press
Melbourne, Vic, Australia

Table of Contents

*To be read by those who go forth by night in the gods'
domain, 2017.*

I am a flame, the son of a flame …
Book of the Dead, Spell 43

As for who reads this book

And who follows its spells

I know your name

You will not die after your death

In Walmart

You will not perish forever

For I know your name

SPELL to Enter Through the Gates of Night.

At a calm time, Saturday morning or Wednesday afternoon, you may be in Walmart, but you have not passed through the GATES OF NIGHT. At a calm time, it's just a store, a woman in a hijab laughing with her husband, Woolite in their cart, America unflavoured. This BOOK is for the dark hours, the seam that ties the end of the evening to sunrise, when the bad, wrong things people do in and around Walmart are a hospital infection, red Rit dye in a load of whites, a gun in a classroom: by the time the problem is identified, it's already ruined everything.

ILLUSTRATION: She registered at Walmart. Her boyfriend served a tour in Iraq and bleeds out of his ear from time to time. He changed his name to Timothy when he returned stateside, but she didn't ask him why. She guesses it was his business. She didn't really want to hear about it, to be honest, and isn't it rude to ask a question you don't want to know the answer to? He got a new Social Security card saying his name is Timothy, then a new driver's license. She didn't go to the DMV with him, because she hates official stuff like that. She never even got a driver's license herself, as much as Mom relies on her to drive, so why should she help someone else get theirs? He has to learn that it's an every-man-for-himself world. She loves him and all but he can't be depending on her too much, and Mom agrees.

A man needs to be a man, each one for himself. He came to pick her from their apartment after he was done at the DMV. He said he wanted to take her to Ruby Tuesday to celebrate his new driver's license. She smoked some weed after he texted to say he was on his way, forgetting that she had already taken a pill she found in the couch. There might have been some mould or something on the weed, or maybe it reacted strange with the pill. On the way to Ruby's, she begged him to turn off the sky. But when he did (by drawing down the sunroof), before her came a sense, nearly visual, of every major good feeling she'd ever had, the excitement of Christmas when she was little, visiting her dad in prison, picking quarters from a jar at Gramma's house, her Disney wedding board on Pinterest: They were as thin and indistinguishable as moth wings, stacked together until her life was done. She huddled inside her misery. She didn't say anything about it to him or anyone. Now she hates the Ruby Tuesday croutons. Before he made the change, his name was Greg. She's due in August.

And Another SPELL Like It.

They've let go the greeters, too expensive. Now armed guards man the doors, more expensive still.

ILLUSTRATION: The part of the wall that holds the guns in Walmart throbs, as if lit differently than anything else on earth, constructed from different particles. People on the other side don't understand. Either that, or they turn away, fearing that, in their heart of hearts, they do. He was once like them, until God lifted the veil from his eyes. He wishes for their sake they are given the grace to hold one, shoot one: let them walk right up to face the power God gave man. It's serious business, a matter of extreme responsibility. He feels about guns the way the hippies who once lived in the trailer next to his felt about LSD. Up until the day they were evicted, they invited him to share their spaghetti dinners and play with their rat. It was actually kind of cute. You wouldn't think a rat could be cute, but it had a really gentle disposition. "I didn't know who I was until I got high," one of them told him. Though he, himself, wasn't comfortable speaking so openly, he believed he knew exactly what she meant. A weightlifter since high school, he hadn't known anything could be so heavy until he held a gun for the first time. It was a Sig Sauer—just a simple, double action handgun, it hadn't even been loaded. He felt the desire to die when he held it, and, buzzing right alongside that desire, the means by which to do so. And when he pulled himself back from choosing to use it like that, the choice he had made felt as physical a thing as pulling a hood from his head. *Our deepest fear is not that we are inadequate*, he read in a meme, *but that we are powerful beyond measure.* He stands with his hands in his pockets, beholding Walmart's wall of guns. At the range this morning, he squeezed the trigger of his PAP M92 and his body absorbed the recoil, pushing out his tendency for thought. Afterward, he took it apart and ran it, piece by piece, under scalding water, to guard against rust. Spread across his dinner table, its great power holds. Miles away from it, he feels its hum.

15

SPELL for Building a Golden Mansion in the Gods' Domain.

It's work. It's war. You have to choose the right thing or else you die. You can step behind the set of a carnival game and win it, but you need to do your research first. You need to push aside the Crest Whitestrips smiles of the tough-guy girl winning her pretty girlfriend a jumbo stuffed alligator. Leave them their dumb fun. You're at work, at war, and you've won.

ILLUSTRATION: Standing in the laundry aisle mourning the price discrepancy of nearly an entire dollar, he rues what a moron he was for buying detergent at the no-name place by his apartment. What was he thinking? He had found himself at the little store and acted rashly, fearing some unexpected need to do a load of wash and him caught, like a fool, with no detergent. But of course he had found no sudden need to do the wash—such a thing had never happened in his life—and now he had at home an unopened container of laundry detergent that he had paid a needless dollar for, a donation to no-name, whose workers are always off somewhere and must be summoned by ringing the bell that sits beside the cash register. While waiting to be waited on, he has, once or twice, considered absconding with whatever he's there for. And he has made himself smile by imagining that he might one day ask, when the young man or woman arrives behind the counter at last, "Do you want my money, or not?" Of course, he wouldn't be so rude; and besides, he is always prepared to pay for what he's getting. He's proud of that. Never used credit in his life. He runs his finances as tightly as the shipshape Little League team he coached to the World Series in 1984, ten years after his own son graduated eighth grade. In the first round of the play-offs, they beat the team that everyone thought would go on to win it all. And he beats his wife, too, but he's pretty sure no one knows. The only person outside his family who could possibly know is a male nurse from the one time they went to the hospital. Fortunately, she only has a slight limp, and, with what he remembers from his associate's degree in anatomy, he's been able to treat most of her wounds himself.

17

SPELL for Living on Air in the Gods' Domain.

Subway has sunken its mystery yeast perfume into thousands of landmarks—university student centres, state-sponsored highway rest stops—but not Walmart; rising up against it, Walmart asserts its industrial-scented air: stronger than you, whoever you are. Stronger than anything inside it, stronger than the smell of Subway, stronger than the vacuum cleaner called SHARK that I want so badly I would sell my husband for it, stronger than the invisible battle behind the handicapped sign that hangs in the window of the busted Toyota Highlander, the happy result of a year-and-a-half-long campaign of letter-writing and telephone conversations with a sympathetic paralegal at a regional Legal Aid office.

ILLUSTRATION: The Bad One takes out the Subway boxes when the sun is on low, at the far side of the sky. You came here from that far place, a world of long, hungry passes that you won't return to, come what may, no matter how fast the trucks here travel or how many nights on end rain falls. The Bad One's boxes are almost always empty, and he tends to pull the Dumpster latch tight. You hear the scrape of his boxes against the ground and your stomach growls, and then you growl, but you know to ignore it. The scant chance for scraps isn't worth being spotted, and so you and everyone scatter into packs of one, imbedded in the amber out-there. You are waiting for the Big One, he who works in darkness. His boxes are carpeted with lettuce, tomatoes, and onions, washed and trimmed. Sometimes you crawl into the Dumpster to get at them (he always leaves it open). But on lucky nights, the Big One piles his boxes beside the Dumpster, so you can walk right up. You like to get there early, when the stars are brightest, biting open the sky. From the margins of the parking lot, you watch him emerge from the double doors of his hiding place, before the sound of cardboard on asphalt brings everyone else running. Once, he piled them up to the moon. It was one of the wildest nights of your life. The whole community feasted. You and your wife stood on top of the pile and howled recklessly. In the high air, hot and still, your fur unruffled, you told the moon that you were beyond its orders—that it would take orders from *you*, and the moon bowed its head in servitude. You left with what you could carry and fed your babies well.

19

SPELL to Light the Path Through Night.

The lamps made by slaves look terrible. The slaves did a terrible job making them. They didn't even bother to fit the shades to the bases—you're just supposed to jam them together. The slaves made pieces of shit. I can't take home a lamp like this. I can't pay $11.97 for this terrible slave lamp. What would my Crate and Barrel bedroom table say?

And Another SPELL Like It.

I don't want to spend eternity with the lights off. I'll buy the most expensive, longest lasting bulbs, and charge them to my Amex.

ILLUSTRATION: She hates the whiney, minor word "want." It doesn't have enough meat on it to describe the ache she feels: *Desire* is more like it, deep and layered as any adult romance. Every night when the light is stripped from the world, she stirs to predict how the next day will cast her desire. Mom and Dad grow taller, their faces further away. They have the power to throw shadows on her chances of ever getting it, or to go online and order it for her this very second. If only she could convince them. Skilfully, they skim the rich, luscious topic from the surface of the conversation. "Well, you'll have to ask Santa for it at Christmas." But it's July! She sifts around inside herself for language sufficiently angry to wield against so belittling a suggestion, but she comes up empty. Empty in the dirty red pit of rage where *desire* lies. Why would God let her desire rise so high without release? In the boring world, the moment has passed. Her parents are on to something else, something unimportant. They've left her alone with her desire. She is an arrow pointed toward it, a whole book about it, a treasure map. She goes down to the basement to watch TV in the hope of catching a commercial for it. She hasn't been watching long enough for a commercial break when Mom calls, "I'm going to Walmart, sweetie!" She hears the jangle of keys. "WAIT!" she cries. "Mom. *Wait*!" She rushes upstairs to put on her shoes, the hot ocean rushing at her ears. Mom says a few things that she is too agitated to even try to hear. Soon, she'll be sharing space with it, standing in front of it, beholding it, touching it. She sighs, setting a cloud on the car window against which she's pressed her head. She is strong, and, God, she can wait, holding steady for however long it takes.

SPELL for Carrying Food and Water Through the Gods' Domain.

What hasn't this shopping cart held? It's the dirtiest thing in the world, jammed into a ragged star with the second, third, fourth, fifth, and sixth dirtiest things, in the middle of the parking lot. Rounded up and slung together every hour or so, these carts don't click into place or make a pattern. They say you don't want to know what's happened in them, so I will turn my face away while it's still innocent.

ILLUSTRATION: He often is asked about his "Walmart Standard" by L1s and people at parties or during the Q&As after lectures. His argument was simple, because his wife had thought of it. This is why he has a wife: To come up with simple arguments that he himself, caught up in the intricacies of legal theory and eschewing what he'll call here daily life, otherwise might miss. He credits certain of his successes to his willingness to consult with her before penning some of his major family-, woman-, and/or domestic-oriented opinions. In layman's terms, the Walmart Standard is that a company known for a certain household or domestic product (it was difficult for him to come up with an example, given his nonparticipation in daily life, but he and his wife finally settled on the well-known company Clorox, with its close identification to household bleach) generally has a greater market-driven incentive to produce an effective product than what is typically called a "store-brand" product (such as, in the example devised, a household bleach produced and distributed by a Walmart corporate partner specifically for the purposes of Walmart in-house retail). This is due to the market reality that, as his wife perspicaciously noted, the Clorox brand is indelibly associated in the consumer mind with household bleach, while the Walmart brand is associated with a large retail environment, as opposed to any non-branded or Walmart-branded item, such as household bleach. Among laymen, he rarely gets into the specifics of the case in which the Walmart Standard was established, but it involved a specious false advertising claim, found such because, he argued for the bench, Walmart advertises but one item: Walmart. To the extent that a specific non- or Walmart-branded item, such as household bleach, malfunctions, the Walmart "brand" bears little negative outcome. Extrapolating the standard for the purposes of consumers, and again in layman's terms, the generic (here "Walmart") product is more likely to malfunction than the "brand name" (here "Clorox") product.

And Another SPELL Like It.

You can take it with you. You can take it with you in a cart,

to where nothing is lost,

and nothing is lost,

and nothing will be lost.

ILLUSTRATION: Her friend says Walmart has an official policy not to stop shoplifters. Well, not actually her friend, but this guy she's chatted with a couple times at the bar next to the cleaners where her sister works. So you can just walk in, get what you need, and walk out, he says. She's tested it, and as long as she doesn't take anything too bulky or unusual, no one side-eyes her as she leaves. She once tried to walk out with a crock pot, but an old ex-cop-type (blond/white/gray buzz cut, his torso the size and shape of a bulletproof vest) stopped her at the exit, saying, "Sweetheart, does that belong to you?" Never meeting his eyes, she turned right around, then disappeared, she hoped, back into the store, where she put the crock pot on some random shelf. She doesn't understand how people live, in a material sense. How do they know what to buy, and where do they get the money? People of the kind her dad used to call "straight," whose apartments magically start smelling like onions in butter at 5 pm every night, and a little while later supper is served at a table set with placemats. That kind of life isn't something you can buy. But it almost is. She chooses a loose pink sweatshirt and walks from the front of the store to the back, which is like walking across a six-lane highway. In a restroom stall, she pulls the tags from the sweatshirt. She peruses the store, depositing into the forgiving sweatshirt a three-pack of navy blue hand towels and two bottles of nail polish. She imagines a messy room in a house, stuffed with crap too big to hide in a sweatshirt—rugs, a desktop computer, a table, reclining chairs, giant candles in wrought-iron candleholders, a toolbox, pillows and down comforters in huge wicker baskets, potted plants, an acoustic guitar, a crock pot.

SPELL for Passing Through the Gods' Domain Undetected.

This is an unnumerology. Forget your ID. Each letter of the alphabet is contained inside itself, without mystery. Props to the great discoveries of the early twentieth century: People can be stacked and sold like those novelty vanity license plate keychains bearing popular first names. Cara, Cari, Carina, Carissa, Carisa, Carla, Carline, Carly, Carole, Carolina, Caroline, Carrie, Carrissa, Carrisa, Cary, Caryn, Caryna, let the machine do it, for I'm only just getting started, and, forgive me, God, I've already missed so much.

ILLUSTRATION: He brings new recruits there and lets them picks out ten items of clothing and three pieces of jewellery, anything they want. It's one of his favourite parts of the job. He loves seeing their eyes light up when he tells them the deal. "It's Christmastime, Girl." He always says that. If he wrote an employee manual, he would probably put that in there, that you're supposed to say that to the girls when you take them to Walmart at the beginning. Of course, there isn't an employee manual, and if there were, Ned would write it, not him, since, as Ned constantly reminds him, Ned is in charge. And yet it's he, not Ned, who goes out in public with the girls to places like Walmart, he who takes risks for their business. The way it works is, he uses cash to buy a couple things he happens to need anyway, and at the cash register, he tells the girl, "Hey! You're really bothering me, you know that? Why don't you go wait in the car?" He prepares the girls for this part, telling them before they go into the store that he's going to yell at them, but that he's not really mad. They're not always the brightest bulbs in the garden, but most of them understand. While the cashier is ogling them, getting invested in the little domestic scene, he puts all the shit the girl picked up in his bag. But now, the store's got these ladies checking your receipt at the door, so they have to basically repeat the same scene again before they leave. Still, it works. Doesn't make him nervous or anything. It's probably the last good time for some of these girls. He feels bad for them, but as he tells his wife, if he started to think about it too much, he wouldn't be able to bring home the bacon. Sometimes he actually gets bacon during these little trips! That always makes them laugh, him and his wife.

27

SPELL for Hopefulness in the Gods' Domain.

Maybe we can turn this whole thing around. Nation states aren't that old. Countries have crumbled to ash in our lifetimes.

ILLUSTRATION: He lets people sleep in their cars in the parking lot. That's official. As in, company policy. He has noticed that people who live in cars in the Walmart lot tend to sleep at night and move around the store during the day. Such schedule of behaviour places minimal additional burden on law enforcement, who face drastically increased incidents of crime in the facility starting at sundown. There's one family, he doesn't like to think of it this way, but it seems like the kids see him almost as a father figure. They have a dad, but the guy spends much more time in the car than the rest of the family. From his observation, most people who sleep in their cars tend to use their cars as sleeping spaces but not living spaces, for reasons related to quality of life, sanitation, and the simple fact that there is very little room in a car. However, this guy really does spend a good deal of each 24-hour period in the vehicle, leading him to guess that there are some drug-related issues here. Initially, he was hesitant to accept this job, but not because he thought it might involve becoming a father-figure-type to a bunch of kids whose families live in cars. If he had known that all this extra emotional stuff would be involved, he never would have taken the job. His reason for hesitating seems comically minor, in retrospect: he didn't want to alternate between first, second, and third shifts. He accepted the position, despite that reservation, because it was a salary bump. He's always taking things from storerooms, the Dumpsters, even the shelves, to give to those kids. There is no tree there, and yet the sense of a shadow falls over the part of the lot where their families keep their cars, never driving them.

SPELL to Maintain One's Class Status in the Gods' Domain.

Most people aren't allowed to touch papyrus. These fingers have never touched a person who's touched it. The eyes these fingers accidentally rub have never seen it. This BOOK was written on a 17-cent limestone notepad lifted from a ten-ton bin of 17-cent limestone notepads, screwed to the ground by slaves in the gods' domain, amen.

ILLUSTRATION: He remembers the precise taste of the particular candy bar he was eating, and stealing by eating, as if it had been lovingly formed by a baker, when the cop tapped him on the shoulder. He would be able to identify it in a line-up of Snickers of varying degrees of being eaten/stolen. Since it was his third strike, he knew this cop, whose beat was Walmart, somewhat well, although she seemed not to know him in the slightest. She was obviously the kind of person to whom *they all look the same*. His first strike had been a folder, with which he had brazenly walked past the receipt-checkers. He hadn't intended to be brazen or even to steal it—it was so insignificant an item that he had just *taken* it, a difficult thing to explain to the officer. He later learned it had cost 17 cents. "Was it worth it?" the cop asked him. He felt like asking her the same thing. His second strike, a CD player, he had paid for dearly, spending the entire night in Walmart's pseudo-jail room because his mom worked the third shift and couldn't find anyone else to pick him up. That was the most embarrassing strike, not only because of his having to stay in the holding cell, but because a CD player seems to him exactly the sort of item that someone who steals would steal. The Snickers, folder, and CD player aren't the only things he's taken, but being caught for the Snickers and the folder was irritating—and absurd. The CD player, because it *wasn't* an absurd thing to steal or be caught for stealing, irritated him all the more. It was a cliché to steal a CD player. Anymore, who even uses a—he couldn't finish that thought, the thought itself being too much of a cliché. And now what will stop him from spinning around inside himself like this, the CD player forced eternally on play, in prison, actual prison, for such victimless crimes?

SPELL to Return One's Memory Back to One in the Gods' Domain.

Download this. It's standard issue, but it'll do as well as what you had. Now, forget this ever happened, and go on as you were.

ILLUSTRATION: You know the song "America"? By Simon and Garfunkel? That song's a lie. He knows that now. Everybody just keeps looking and looking for it and they die like that, in their car with their lover in traffic on the turnpike. What once seemed romantic is now pathetic. He thought he would just keep being young. He beholds in confusion the Facebook pages of his friends. Why would they want to keep jobs? marry one another or, worse, strangers? dab each others' pages with reminders to come to dinner? They play board games and subscribe to some sort of service that posts the results of those games to their timelines. He looks out the window of the room he rents, thinking of the university he attended. He hadn't attended it, really. He had just crashed for a year in the dorm of his friend who was a student there. But he had gone to a few classes. The second semester he was there, he took an Oceanography course all the way through. He didn't take the final or anything, but he went to nearly every lecture. Sometimes he'd be sitting there, watching the clock like the real students, with its red second-hand that moved like an oar through water, and he would think, what am I doing? I could get up and leave.

And then he would think, so could they. Nobody ever did. He promised his roommate he would stop by Walmart today and pick up the stuff they need for their apartment. He has been promising to do this for several days. It seemed so possible this morning, but now, the greyness of the day has set in, and he knows he won't do it. What should he do, sign up for OKCupid? Apply to the community college? The day is already over. He hears Charles's key in the lock and feels a fleeting sense of homesickness for his childhood. He'll never again be a kid waiting for his mom to come home from work. That time, like so many others, is gone.

SPELL to Shed One's Ideology in the Gods' Domain.

You shouldn't have tried so hard to get that handi-capped sign. You should have lain down where you stood and let the present wash over you like the tide tickling the sand in Hawaii in an ad for tampons during a commercial break on *The Bachelorette*. If it doesn't matter to Walmart, it shouldn't matter to you.

ILLUSTRATION: He's basically the king of the elec-tronics area. He doesn't mean to brag, but life is good. If you can't live on the salary they're giving you here, that's on you. He makes the same as the other guys, and he lives in his own apartment, a condo, with two televisions, one of which offers a 4K viewing expe-rience. That one he purchased with his employee discount. He bought the other at Best Buy, because he didn't want to take advantage of Walmart by making too many large purchases with his employee discount. He'll do that occasionally, shop elsewhere, although he knows Walmart has the best prices. For example, he'll often buy cosmetics, like shampoo and conditioner, at the CVS by his condo, for the sake of convenience, it being so close to where he lives, and also so as not to abuse his Walmart employee discount. However, he knows that Walmart has the freshest produce, so he picks up groceries there a couple times a week after his shift. He pulled himself up by his bootstraps by starting in grocery and working his way into electronics, increasing his hourly salary by, well, it would be rude to say how much, so he'll just say a lot. Sometimes, he actually does end up telling people how much he makes, but only customers he has developed a relationship with, by serving them on either multiple occasions or for an extended period of time on a single occasion—for example, if they're making a large purchase, like a television. To be honest, he's not entirely sure that Walmart has the freshest produce. Once, when he was still in grocery, he opened a box of potatoes that were all soft and mouldy, and his supervisor told him to put them out on the floor. But that could have been an aberration. Anyway, nothing like that would ever happen in electronics.

SPELL for Not Eating Shit in the Gods' Domain.

Hungry though I may be—

Starving though I may be—

I will not: touch nor take shit into my mouth.

But, say the Gods, we have blended it in a Frappucino, we have tested it in a lab, where a special state-of-the-art dry pasteurization method was designed with your safety and the safety of your family in mind. It is on the menu at McDonald's, where the drive-thru line grows long with orders for it. The wealthiest among us sit at the tables in the coffee shop, gazing at their Macs, and break off bits of it without looking. They maintain their slender, strong physiques, without seeming to try. They kiss each other with sour-scented breath. What say you? demand the Gods.

Hungry though I may be—

Though I may be cast out from the others—

Starving though I maybe be—

Though I may be the one unkissed among them—

I will not: touch nor take shit into my mouth.

My abomination is my abomination. I will not touch it with my hands, nor step on it with the soles of my boots. My nourishment comes from a bar wrapped in sterile plastic in a factory in China and shipped across the trade-war-riven sea. I open my mouth to that bar alone. I will not eat shit.

ILLUSTRATION: They come to pick up their medicine and then they leave. But she remains, suffering. From whatever they arrive and are spit out back to, those individual workplace hells would tremble before the suffering she endures. "Girly!" He cries from the back. He doesn't interface with the public. "Yessir?" she utters. He doesn't respond, and she doesn't follow up. He might be revving up for a long speech, or perhaps he is distracted by his own meanderings. She wouldn't presume to know. She knows nothing except her servitude to him, a knot that only ever gets tighter. He tells her how lucky she is—does she know how hard it is for convicted felons to get jobs? and here she is squandering this excellent opportunity. She regards the line curling into the body wash aisle. He allows her one restroom break per shift, and demands a detailed oral report on what he calls her "end product" when she returns. Being essentially nonphysical, this is one of the lesser of his assaults. "Taking my restroom break, Sir!" she calls. She lets go the latch on the half-door before he can reply. She will pay later for this act of insubordination. Out in the free, open store, outside of his influence, the ceiling is three times higher and the air is pure. People stop her on her way to the bathroom— innocents, thick in their bubbles of unknowing. Excuse me, where's the kitchen stuff at? Kin you tell

37

me where is the garbage cans? Ma'am, markers? She is too bereft of connection to attend to them. She has no advice for anyone. And so, against company policy, and throwing to the wind the week of orientation and testing she received, she tells them, I don't know, I work in pharmacy. She gestures, for proof, to her t-shirt, on which is pinned her "pharmacy assistant" tag, shaped like a tombstone.

SPELL to Go Forth in Triumph in the Gods' Domain.

Mission Accomplished. The banner flapped against the airplane, a meme. But this was an emblem of the disaster in the middle of happening. If you had been in it, inside it, a part of it…. Now, when they say the world will end, whatever the gods have planned, well, let's just say that you would be among the ones who knew it was coming. And who knew how you'd react when it came.

ILLUSTRATION: Read Marx, said his friend who went to college. So he Googled "The Communist Manifesto," but the words bled together. They slipped down the screen. He would pay someone to read it for him or to him if he had money. The thought falls away. He squats to lift another pair of boxes into the truck. There's a hard way to do it and an easy way to do it, and, unfortunately, the hard way is better for your back. It sounds gay to say it, but the work is really lonely. There are a bunch of guys who, like him, move boxes, and none of them bothered to tell him that you get in trouble when you listen to headphones. The large-scale noises of the floor—the tractor's hiss as it uncouples from its trailer, a pack of pallets hitting the ground with a hard FUCK sound—reach the ear as an assertive silence. He was eager to drown it out with Gucci Mane. The other guys on the floor watched him put on his headphones the afternoon of the first day, then again in the mid-morning of the second day, then again at the beginning of the third day, immediately after which the floor manager marched down from the loft-style second floor, where he surveyed the men at work from his desk. "D'you wanna git killed? No? No? You can't hear a truck back up with them things on! C'mon!" The floor manager was still shaking his head as he walked back to the stairs, his high-heeled boots making a variety of different sounds on the numerous materials he traversed. At the base of the stairs, however, he turned around with a different face, as if having finished his part in a play. He wasn't angry at all anymore, merely curious. "Ain't nobody told you not to use them things?"

SPELL to Not Let a Man's Truck Be Taken From Him in the Gods' Domain.

Into the bed of which he placed his boots, soles facing up, every day of his working life on earth.

In which he pulled up to the light beside the construction zone on the corner of Johnston and Camelia and leaned out the open passenger-side window and said, "Heyyyy…" to me in my car as I stared straight ahead, pretending it wasn't happening.

From which he speaks,

I row through the night in my chariot

Once unrecognized as a God

I now teach Gods their names

41

ROLL of Gods.

To Be Said By Those Who Enter the Gods' Domain.

O broad gods of the hall of truth, I have ascended unto you, I am among you, here, I live on truth, truth like you, and I know your names—

O patron of the only independent bookstore in a two-hundred-mile radius, I have not wasted my time.

O installer of the hardwood bamboo flooring that turned out to cause cancer in 80% of rats exposed to it in the lab, I have not lived in vain.

O invader of Iraq, who came forth from the board-room, I have not worn someone else's boots.

O Dominick Dunne, who came forth from *Vanity Fair* to cover the O.J. Simpson trial, I have not brought any man's daughter to harm.

O amateur photographer looking into the windows of the apartment building next door, who came forth from the gods' domain, I have not dared disturb the universe.

O alligator-skinned yet sexy guide of swamp tours on the Atchafalaya, who came forth from the gods' domain, I have not been unchaste.

O gargoyle nested in a crevice of Bond Chapel, I have not taken more than my share.

O conserver of our nation's natural resources, I have gone to bed at a reasonable hour.

O biologist scraping the cells from algae, I have not intervened in matters that weren't my business.

O brokers of fragile peace treaties, I've never made a joke at the airport.

O grocery store cheque writer, who made longer the endless line, who came forth from the gods' domain, I have not rammed my cart against the cart in front of it, creating a riot.

O maintenance man of the apartment complex, who seems to just Google how to fix whatever is broken, which we could just do ourselves, who came forth from the gods' domain, I have sought to control my temper.

O maintenance man of the apartment complex, who made a huge mess in our apartment, who came forth from the gods' domain, I admit to having yelled a little bit when I got home, but you yelled a lot and then gave a long, still yelling, monologue about "life."

O maintenance man of the apartment complex, who stormed out after that, leaving the mess you made, who came forth from the gods' domain, that particular time I did not seek to control my temper, but at other times, I have sought to control my temper.

O maintenance man of the apartment complex, in CVS later with a strung-out woman and a baby, I was about to say hello, but when I saw that you didn't want me to, I averted my eyes.

O maintenance man of the apartment complex, who came forth from the gods' domain, how could I presume to know what you want?

O maintenance man of the apartment complex, whom when I mention, a shadow falls over my husband's handsome face, I have not been violent.

O maintenance man of the apartment complex, who came forth from the gods' domain, in my daily heart, I hate you.

O maintenance man, who came forth from the gods' domain, my husband beholds you mildly, saying hey man.

O maintenance man, who came forth from the gods' domain, my hate for you jumps to my husband, ruining everything: Why is he so nice to you and so mean to me?

O maintenance man of the apartment complex, walking down the block with twin toddlers in a double stroller three miles from the apartment complex at 4 am on Saturday night or Sunday morning, whatever you want to call it, who came forth from the gods' domain, I have struggled at the foothills of your existence.

O maintenance man of the apartment complex, who came forth from the gods' domain, far more than I hate you, I fear you.

O friend of my youth, I have not been garrulous.

O wives of my ex-boyfriends, I have not wept.

O amateur marathoner who shares his training data on Facebook, I have not reviled the gods.

O hikers who crossed the line between Iran and Iraq, one of whom I went to camp with as a child, the other two who got engaged during their captivity and whom I know nothing else of, who came forth from the gods' domain, I have not judged too harshly.

O harpist at a "laidback, unfussy" wedding covered in the *Times*' Vows column, who came forth from the gods' domain, I have not given my love lightly.

O Uber driver working overnight on an impossibly busy holiday, I have not despaired when there was still a drop of hope left in the jar.

O reporter for the *Hyde Park Herald*, who came forth from the gods' domain, I have not been cruel.

O roofer, who came forth from the gods' domain, I have not thought of my perspective as the only one.

O valet who fears people think he drives their cars dangerously as soon as he slides out of sight, but who actually does do that, who came forth from the gods' domain, I have not wasted my youth.

O nurse at the bed of the dying on a towel on a bed in the suburbs, I was not sullen.

O singer of the national anthem at a minor league night game, I have not said yes when I meant no.

O inventor of this millennium, who came forth from Silicon Valley, I did not profit from the Internet.

O rabbi who came forth from either Sinai or Akiba Shector, I can't remember which one is which, I'm pretty sure I have not insulted the God in my heart.

O prospectors, I have not sought to travel where I know I won't be welcome.

O shoppers, who came forth from the gods' domain, I have not budged in line.

O shoppers, who came forth from the gods' domain, to be totally honest, I budged in line a few times, but rarely.

O Britney Spears, who came forth from the gods' domain, I have scorned to change my state with kings.

O greeters, who came forth from the gods' domain, I have looked my fellow man in the eye.

O greeters, who came forth from the gods' domain, I have run my eye over the bodies of my fellow man, but I have done so briefly, and as surreptitiously as possible.

O professors, scholars, administrators of knowledge, who came forth from the gods' domain, I have not told a lie. And every lie I told was true.

To Know the Names of Those Who Are at the Seven Gates of the Gods' Domain, Their Guardians and Announcers.

1ˢᵗ Gate.

The name of its doorkeeper is Maker of the Crock Pot You Bought Even Though You Didn't Want It And Now Are Waiting in Line to Return Because It Didn't Work. The name of its guardian is Ever-Questioner; the name of the voice on the loudspeaker is Panicker.

To be said by the dead on arriving at this gate: I am patient, experienced, I have been in pain. I have stood for hours during meetings, counting the tiles on the ceiling, on days I forgot my phone. Stand aside and let me pass.

2ⁿᵈ Gate.

The name of its doorkeeper is Climate Changer. The name of its guardian is Flood-Face; the name of the voice on the loudspeaker is Too Late.

To be said on arriving at this gate: Stand aside: I've foretold all. I've already begun to miss the earth, our home. I practiced missing the cars of my childhood, scrubbed from the streets as if by conspiracy before my 20s were done. Rabbits, tiny Toyota Camrys, VW Bugs, Volvo station wagons, Oldsmobiles perforating the cold and over Chicago nights.

3rd Gate.

The name of its doorkeeper is Imprisoner. The name of its guardian is Executioner; the name of the voice on the loudspeaker is Darkness, Silence, and Fear Forever.

To be said by the dead on arriving at this gate: Oh Lord, do not let me be like Albert Woodfox, 43 years in solitary in Angola Prison for nothing—*nothing*—nothing, who I thought about every day for several weeks, then thought of no more until hearing he would be released; meanwhile, all that time he kept living, had been living all along, and lives still. And Lord, do not let me be like Haleh Esfandiari, who in 2007 went to visit her ailing mother in Iran and was accused of being a spy and put in the Evin Prison, a scholar, a journalist, an activist for the freedom of women throughout the world. And Lord, do not let me be like my dad's client, a philanthropic Democrat who ran a fleet of regional food service vehicles, sent to Cook County Prison for 11 months after a sham trial brought by the Republican-led USDA.

4th Gate.

The name of its doorkeeper is Pretender. The name of its guardian is Facebook, the name of the voice on the loudspeaker is Giving It Away For Free.

To be said by the dead on arriving at this gate: Every day was wasted.

5ᵗʰ Gate.

The name of its doorkeeper is the College You Did or Didn't Graduate From. The name of its guardian is the Place You Work, the name of the voice on the loudspeaker is the Secret Websites You Seek and What You Want to Find There.

To be said by the dead on arriving at this gate: But that was not my life. None of that was me. Lord, drop me back down there and let me try again. Censor from their mouths any mention of me, it isn't true. I wasn't this or that, I am the gyre inside myself, unmanned, Lord, please let me go again.

6ᵗʰ Gate.

The name of its doorkeeper is Money. The name of its guardian is Pictures of Beautiful Things, the name of the voice on the loudspeaker is All I Bought and Owned.

To be said by the dead on arriving at this gate: Lord, please. Don't tell me anything. I wouldn't necessarily have chosen it, but the available options were few. So I activated the Domino's Pizza Tracker, Googled how exactly payday loans work, picked through a bin of discounted moisturizers at CVS, signed up for free trials that I forgot to cancel and am still paying $9.99 a month for. I stand before you, Lord, puzzling over whether to buy the yeast infection test or to go right for the yeast infection treatment, because what if it turns out not to be a yeast infection? But Lord, what if it *is* a yeast infection? What then? If you're such a God, Lord, answer that: What then?

7th Gate.

The name of its doorkeeper is the Maintenance Man of the Apartment Complex's Name. The name of its guardian is Why Didn't You Even Bother to Learn His Name, the name of the voice on the loudspeaker is Your Hatred.

To be said by the dead on arriving at this gate: Hail to you, maintenance man of my apartment complex. *Look, he's been here all night*, my husband said of you. *He works hard.* And I said, he's *at* work, but that doesn't mean he's working hard. Even as I face my doom, I smile to remember. I, who is neither at work a lot nor works hard, standing in the narrow lane of myself. Please, please, please, please, *please* don't report my wickedness to the other gods. May you tell the Truth for me before the Lord of the Universe, for I have done what was right in Chicago, IL, St. Louis, MO, Ann Arbor, MI, Fairfax, VA, and Lafayette, LA, and on the highway between them, I beg you, *please*.

And Another Like It.

Listen, what is your name? Or I will, like the others, as I pass you simply say *hey*. I already have diffused my hatred, like robots working on a bomb in Central Park. No affair of mine has come before the authorities, and whenever I was pulled over, I burst into tears quite naturally, and then I was released.

SPELL for Not Dying Again in the Gods' Domain.

I have already died again once I was already dead, and so, oh Lord, do not let me die again when I die again. I rode the circle death is. I was the One, the only rider left on the Ferris wheel when it snagged, and I was stuck at the highest point for an entire generation. I died there, and died again inside myself while I waited those years in my dead body to go back down to earth. My death held my life like a bead in a scarab. Let this be the last trip, once and for all, Lord, let me rest in this ending.

ILLUSTRATION: He is 40 but looks 8,000. He's killed a person but it wasn't his fault, and some people kill many people. He didn't mean to. He's not like an actual killer, with bad intentions and a desire for harm. Not like someone in a movie. It's nothing like that. People out of history or in other countries have killed hundreds, even thousands. He's not like that—nothing like that. It's not like he did it on purpose. This is why he never thinks about it. It just leads to guilty associations. Sometimes you end up doing things without intending to. How was he supposed to know the guy was so weak? He probably would have died that day no matter what happened—when your time is up, it's up. He shouldn't have put himself at risk like that, being so weak. He had crumpled up like a beer can. There was an empty, casual feeling in the loose minutes, maybe just one or two, until the police cars and ambulance arrived. That feeling ended abruptly. If it had been him, if he were the one who was so weak, he never would have put himself at risk like that. He would have treated himself like a baby bird, gentle as could be. And anyway, shoplifting is what's illegal, not stopping shoplifters, so he has nothing to feel bad about. That's what the jury said, and the judge agreed. That's why he never thinks about it. The jury, every last one of them, said it was manslaughter, which, as his lawyer explained, basically means you didn't do it. That's why he didn't get any punishment. But it's funny how being free to come back to work, here where he did it, is sort of a punishment of its own.

SPELL for Not Being Stuck Alone in an Alternate Dimension Forever.

Lord, I am not the one on whom you zapped down that twilight, right? the way of seeing that pulls out in front and behind me, stretching as far as I don't want or need: I knew that was the last night of my life; and so, knowing it isn't mine, I fold it (I remember the streaks of sunset, like rips in the canvas of the world), hasty, a little disgusted, like when someone else's underpants get in my laundry.

ILLUSTRATION: The remedy sort of revived him. He is kind of alive. Immediately afterward, his parents had checked him out of the hospital and set him up in an apartment on University Avenue, near where he had been living, long ago, when he had started college. But by then, he seems to remember, he was already too far gone. He never would have had any kind of upright life. Who would have had him start college? Maybe, on second thought, that was from a film he saw. He eats a giant bowl of cereal and then walks once around the block with his cane. These two activities take all day, for he is severely compromised, both mentally and physically. How can it be that his parents have been advised to let him live like this? What sort of expert would sanction such a situation? He is truly alone. But he did something horrible, something very upsetting that, luckily, he can't remember. Maybe, on second thought, he isn't alone. He seems to have a couple roommates, shapes moving in and out of view at morning and night. As he walks down the block, his death is dangling ahead of him, in the middle of his vision. It looks like a sock. His ability for sight is temporary, someone told him as he was being wheeled out of the hospital. He might have been told this a few times prior, as well. A crushing sense of loss walks slowly toward him. It looks like the funny monster in *Spaceballs*, the thing made out of cheese. He simply moves aside, and in that way is able to avoid it. With a start, he sees that he is missing part of his foot. There is the tired feeling of pressing a button he's pressed before, which tells him the issue of the missing foot has been dealt with. Relief washes over him and he pees. It feels wonderful. He still has half the block to go. He's exhausted. Mom and Dad set up his apartment with stuff they got at Walmart, the giant bowls he eats his cereal in. Why did they gets such big bowls? On second thought, Dad wasn't there; it was only Mom. Dad is not a part of the world anymore. He can't remember. Maybe, on second thought, he was there.

SPELL for Making One Not Have to Work in the Gods' Domain.

Save my settings, save my settings, Lord, or I might as well not pass through. Nothing could interest me in the Heavens like what I watched on television. My love is shallow, up against how deeply I was entertained. The way I left myself behind—that became who I was.

ILLUSTRATION: He has a t-shirt featuring an airbrushed image of Donald Trump, looking slim and belligerent, standing on a tank. He's proud of his lack of education. Anti-education, he calls it. He doesn't care what happens. The world is already over. Anything could happen and he'd simply endure. His wife drops him off at Walmart at 10 am. The earlier part of the morning is reserved for the café, where he socializes with a few veterans of the first Gulf War, who he never forgets to thank for their service, even though they did deskwork, but still. His time at Walmart he spends browsing tools. He hasn't made as many friends there as he has at the café. This is because some of the people at Walmart are rude, especially in the manlier sections, like plumbing and automotive. He tries to ignore them. At noon, his wife or son will pick him up and take him home for lunch. After that he naps, then watches his programs. It's important to keep busy. That's why his wife, for example, works. Work has never appealed to him, and he has problems with authority, which is one of the reasons he doesn't get along well with some of the people at Walmart. Another thing that keeps him from working, as he discovered when he sought work a couple years ago, at the urging of first his wife, then his son, is his anti-education. At the time, his son had told him, using harsh language that he will not repeat, that it wasn't fair for everybody in the family to work but him. Life isn't fair, buddy, he should have said, but he didn't think of it at the time. He shakes his head with a sense of gentle wisdom in his imagination, saying life isn't fair, buddy, life isn't fair.

SPELL for Passing Along the Land Route.

I am the one who gives a man indifference, tapping people on the shoulder asking them for a dollar because I seriously just ran out of gas and I'm not at all a drug addict, I honestly swear that I just ran out of gas and if I could just get a single one of the uncounted dollars sleeping in your wallet, none which means anything to you, I could turn my life around, *please*.

And Another SPELL Like It.

This smooth, scuffed tile would be the floor of a palace in another country, in another time.

ILLUSTRATION: Excuse me, excuse me, excuse me, sir! Excuse me, ma'am! He says politely, stepping widely aside. Years of practice, endless trial and error experiments, have resulted in this mix: a courtesanly pre-apology for absolutely nothing while relinquishing space. And he smiles, making eye contact, not in a creepy way, but as often as possible, with whoever he passes, conveying his personhood in a subtle yet assertive manner. But never too assertive, oh, God, no, for he knows where that road leads. He drains his voice of any hint of sarcasm, filling it back up with a sense of joy, real joy, that would lead anyone who heard him to remember him, at a funeral or in an obituary, as someone who "loved his life." Oh, excuse me! He steps kindly aside for a slow-motion, seven-person family. He bows very slightly to each of them, even the children. No one is going to shoot him. No one in this fucking garbage dump is going to take away his innocent black unarmed life. And if they do, his death will be different, his wife will make sure of that. She'll see that the news is splashed across the front pages of the papers these lobotomized country shoppers have never heard of, the *Washington Post*, *The New York Times*, his kids will spray hashtags across the planet, making of him a monument, his dog will bark all night for its owner, piercing the hearts of those who seem heartless, his cat will prowl the neighbourhood, fighting to maim in his memory. He stands aside for another enormous family, smiling, smiling, bending slightly at the knees and waist. And he, he will come back from the dead like Beloved and haunt them, consign them forever to Hell.

SPELL for Passing Through the Sky.

It's up to you how low you want to go. As for me, I think I found the eye in the centre of the scarab at the core of the earth. They always check your ticket, scan you, make sure you've got no liquids. I've passed through once already, so I knew to hold my ticket in my hand.

ILLUSTRATION: If he had finished high school, he might know the words that describe how deeply he doesn't want to be there. The words that would explain why, when there are four minutes left on the clock and the shift supervisor, who insists on calling himself the key holder, although there is no key, just a gate with a lock they all know the combination to that putatively separates the Subway from Walmart, although the Subway is contained within Walmart, says that he can go, but he won't get paid for the last half hour if he does, he gratefully accepts the key holder's offer. He would die if he stayed, so he takes the $3.65 reduction in his paycheque. "Suit yourself!" says the shift supervisor/key holder, as if he had something to gain from the transaction. If he ever gets out of this situation, he promises himself, he will never go into a Subway again. He will never go into an actual subway, he adds, smiling against the tide of his misery. He has only been on a subway once, during a school trip to Chicago in ninth grade. He can draw a straight line from then to now, the same responsibilities pulling at him. He and Deanna were already together by that Chicago trip. When he gets home from work, rather than playing with his daughters or listening to her talk about her day, he plays World of Warcraft. He would be a better husband and father, more like the men on TV, if he didn't have to spend his days at Subway. But that doesn't seem possible, as he has been working at this Subway since it opened inside of Walmart, spontaneously, like a spot of mould on cheese, where once was nothing.

SPELL for Patience in the Gods' Domain.

Here I am. Long do I stand, long do I stand and wait without distraction or purpose, past civility, seeing past what I think the Lord means for us to see, past reason. The endless papyrus of the afterlife doesn't register a single pleat.

ILLUSTRATION: Nowadays, nowadays, nowadays, every sentence he says begins. Young people have no sense of responsibility. Yet it is he who doesn't look up from his phone when his baggy wife asks him to bring home fill-in-the-blank. There's a "Game Centre" button that offers all sorts of distractions. And now he can't remember what it was she wanted, because he was playing in the Game Centre at the time of her request. She'll give him hell when he gets home tonight without whatever it is. Vaseline, maybe? On the other hand, she needs to lay the hell off him. He isn't here to shop for her. In dignity, he straightens a bit in his seat. Long ago, he was a greeter; he now moves an electric wheelchair around the checkout area, motioning toward the shortest lines. "That one's free!" he calls to whoever will catch his eye. He rarely accesses the Game Centre while he's working the floor, and he is open to helping anyone find the best line. It doesn't matter if it's a nice-looking lady with her two kids or any of the other kinds of people they got around here, he'll help. His supervisor is a Negro, but that's fine. He suffered worse indignities in the years after his accident, during which he went without work, waiting hungrily for his wife's pay cheque. This was when he first discovered the Game Centre, like a secret portal, on the cellular phone he had owned and ignored for years. He had been reluctant to file for disability, because he didn't want to be associated with all those people he heard about who lie on the sofa all day, scrounging off the government. It was 18 months after the accident before he filed his first claim, and he only did it then because his wife kept getting her hours cut. Again earning his pay, he tries not think of those years. It is nowadays, the good and bad spun together like a choc/van soft serve cone, and he will take what is owed him.

SPELL: Standing in Line in the Gods' Domain.

Catalogue of CARS,

GODS,

SCHOOLS.

Catalogue of CATALOGUES,

SNACKS,

QUARTERBACKS.

This is the OTHER SIDE. The world is woven together loosely, from particles of night. Through the gaps in the fabric, you see too much. It's too late to close your eyes. Driving around, you're unnoticeable to anyone. If you say your piece when nobody's listening, your turn won't swing round again.

SPELL to be Spoken by Osiris, God of the West: Ruler of the Realm of the Dead.

I am the one who derives substance from Dumpsters.

I irrigate the highways.

I smooth the potholed back roads where men brushed with moles and bruises sit on porches in any weather doing nothing their whole lives long.

Hear me!

Living is work. Lying on the couch after work is work. Sitting in the break room waiting to clock in, the clock has already started. The air in the room smells of the meal last microwaved. We, the Gods, are *working*,

rowing among the stars,

playing chess,

waiting to be beheld.

And Another SPELL like it.

FOR THE GOD OF THE WEST TO SAY.

I will be reverent to none, no God, no being alive or dead.

I travel on foot, the swirls on the soles of my sandals long since rubbed away. I have water; I am equipped.

I open the Otherworld that I may see my father and drive away darkness. Here come I to tap for as long as it takes to get an answer at the hard wall of darkness: O all you gods and all you spirits, prepare a path for me. I have opened up every path in the sky and on the lake and on the highway, for I am the critical-thinking child of my father, Bill Biederman. Open the darkness, I'm coming through.

65

I know your name in Walmart

You will not die after your death

You will not perish forever

For I know your name

Acknowledgements

This book relies on Thomas George Allen's 1960 gloss of the Oriental Institute Museum's holdings and the 2015 Ogden Goelet and R.O. Faulker translation of the Papyrus of Ani. I also drew on *The Quest for Immortality: Treasures of Ancient Egypt*, edited by Betsy M. Bryan and Eric Hornung. Thank you: Brian Gaudino, Pat Schulman, Sam Biederman, Felix Biederman, Marjorie Biederman, Jennifer Morrison, Tyler Mills, Traci Brimhall, Jennifer Atkinson, Eric Pankey, Dayana Stetco, Tricia Gonzales, Daniel D'Angelo.

Vine Leaves Press

Enjoyed this book?
Go to *vineleavespress.com* to find more.